Criminal

He Does Not Confess

The author acknowledges the use

Author's Note

This story began its life as a movie script—purely imaginative and initially crafted to deliver cinematic highs. In the process of transforming it into a novel, the narrative naturally slowed, allowing space for reflection, silence, and psychological depth that the written form demands.

I acknowledge the assistance of artificial intelligence during the development and refinement of this work. The ideas, characters, and moral questions, however, remain my own.

I hope you find something meaningful in this story—whether in its restraint, its questions, or its quiet tensions.

Thank you for reading.

— **Nanda**

Characters

Sanjay
The protagonist. A quiet, observant man shaped by prolonged injustice, silence, and social exclusion. He learns to understand power not through rebellion, but through restraint, documentation, and emotional control.

Sanjay's Father
A principled and hardworking man whose integrity becomes a liability in a corrupt system. His loss of ancestral property marks the beginning of Sanjay's long moral awakening.

Sanjay's Mother
A woman wounded by rumor and humiliation. Her suffering, endured without protest, becomes the emotional core of Sanjay's transformation.

Anaya
Sanjay's romantic interest. Independent and pragmatic, she represents emotional imbalance and unreciprocated affection, revealing Sanjay's growing detachment from personal relationships.

Rama Rao
A relative involved in the inheritance dispute. His actions expose how legality can be manipulated to legitimize injustice.

Endowment / Revenue Officials
Representatives of institutional authority. They embody procedural power, corruption, and the silent mechanisms that favor influence over truth.

Neighbors and Colleagues
Collective voices of society—spreading rumors, passing judgments, and reinforcing silence through passive complicity.

Chapter One

Inheritance of Silence

The house woke before light but without movement. Air lingered in the rooms as if it had learned the shape of waiting. Sanjay stood barefoot in the bathroom, the tiles cold under his feet, the mirror dulled by years of steam that never fully cleared. He looked at his own face as if it belonged to someone he had agreed to watch over. His eyes were steady. His mouth did not move for a long moment.

You are carrying it again, he said finally, not aloud enough to travel beyond the glass. Not loudly enough to ask for mercy. The mirror returned his words without alteration. He nodded once, as if a fact had been confirmed.

From the front room came the sound of paper turning. It was unhurried, precise. His father was already at the table.

The wooden table stood near the window where the morning light entered without warmth. Files lay in measured stacks, their edges aligned with care that bordered on ritual. Irrigation reports, land records, notices stamped and restamped by offices that demanded obedience more than truth. A steel tumbler of tea cooled beside his father's elbow. Outside, the street was empty except for a dog sniffing at the gutter, indifferent to the day assembling itself above.

Before the marriage, this table had belonged to more than one house. Decisions passed through it before they reached anywhere else. Land disputes found their endings here. When water schedules failed and boundaries blurred, when signatures were required in rooms that smelled of dust and impatience, it was this man who went. He returned late, the scent of files and heat clinging to his clothes, and sat again, continuing work others had learned to leave untouched.

The joint family house stood a few streets away, older, broader, its walls thick with years that never fully settled. Sanjay remembered walking its corridors as a child, the ceiling fans stirring warm air that carried voices lowered at the right moments. His father was spoken to easily then. Advice was requested without hesitation. Responsibility arrived and stayed, unchallenged. It did not feel like sacrifice. It felt like order.

The marriage came without drama. A modest hall, chairs aligned, flowers arranged to meet expectation rather than desire. His mother's hands were steady as she adjusted the pleats of her sari. She smiled at people who smiled back and believed, then, that clarity of intention was protection enough. She did not know how quietly stories could be rearranged.

Afterward, the rooms remained unchanged, but they learned new silences. Conversations shortened. Requests arrived later, sometimes not at all. Files that once came naturally now paused elsewhere before finding their way to the table. Responsibility did not leave at once. It thinned. It began to require explanation.

In family meetings, language softened while intent sharpened. His father's efficiency was discussed as ambition. Familiarity with documents became control. Years of unpaid labour were reframed as preparation for personal gain. His mother's presence hovered at the edge of every sentence, unnamed yet central, as if her existence alone required accounting.

When the division of property arrived, it did so dressed in legality. Measurements were taken under the sun. Advocates murmured into phones. Documents passed between hands that no longer hesitated. What his father received was small and exact, a few acres of agricultural land that demanded proof even to remain with him. The rest moved smoothly into other names. No one mentioned gratitude. No one recalled years carried without question.

The court buildings were cold in the mornings and oppressive by noon. Sanjay remembered the benches, the chipped paint, the way dust settled on shoes polished for respect that never arrived. The land waited through hearings and adjournments, indifferent to the struggle around it. When the papers finally aligned with truth, winning felt less like victory than permission to continue.

The house that followed rose slowly, brick by brick, funded by loans that marked time in installments. Each payment was made on schedule. Each receipt was kept. The house did not inherit memory. It accumulated effort. It stood apart from the joint family, visible yet excluded, close enough to remind, distant enough to ignore.

Rumours did not arrive as accusations. They arrived as pauses. As concern shaped into suggestion. His mother's name entered conversations gently, carried on breath that pretended care. Why had his father changed. Why had harmony fractured. Why had things become difficult after marriage. No sentence completed itself. Repetition did the rest.

His father did not answer. He returned each evening, removed his shoes, washed his hands, and sat at the table. Retirement came without ceremony. The files reduced. The waking remained early. Responsibility, once central, became invisible.

At night, Sanjay returned to the mirror. The house slept lightly around him. He studied his reflection as if it were a document that needed verification.

They changed the story, he said. He waited. They punished capability. He waited again. They used silence.

The mirror did not argue. It did not forgive. It held his face without judgment.

I will not forget, he said. Not loudly. Not as a promise. As a record.

He turned off the light and stepped back into the room. Outside, the street settled into routine. Inside, memory arranged itself carefully, learning where it would stay.

Chapter Two

Weather After the Wedding

The first place Sanjay noticed the change was not the joint family house but the road leading away from it. The street looked the same, lined with trees that dropped leaves without pattern, but the walk back felt longer. Sounds followed him farther than before. A door closing echoed too clearly. Laughter from inside a house lingered in a way it had not earlier. He could not have explained it then, only felt that something once shared had shifted position and was now watching from a distance.

The wedding had passed without rupture. It was remembered later as simple, almost uneventful. Chairs had been arranged in straight lines. The priest spoke with practiced calm. Relatives arrived, offered smiles, adjusted jewellery, and spoke in voices trained to sound appropriate. There was no visible protest. No one left early. No one created a scene worth recounting.

His mother stood beside his father with a composure that came naturally to her. She had not grown up in a family that performed authority loudly. Her manner was quiet, deliberate, shaped by years of learning how not to demand space. She believed that kindness, once proven, would be enough. She believed that a family that accepted her into ceremony would eventually accept her into truth.

For a few weeks after the marriage, things appeared unchanged. His father continued leaving early, returning late. He still visited offices. He still attended meetings. He still received phone calls asking for clarification, guidance, intervention. The joint family house remained accessible. Doors were open. Meals were shared. Words were exchanged.

But tone began to drift.

In conversations, pauses appeared where none had existed. Questions were asked twice, then left unanswered. Advice was sought and then followed selectively. His father noticed it first in small matters. A decision delayed without reason. A document reviewed by someone else before it reached him. A suggestion received with nods and later dismissed as unnecessary.

Nothing was said openly. That was the method. No confrontation meant no responsibility.

His mother sensed it differently. She noticed how often conversations shifted rooms when she entered. How compliments were phrased with effort, as if carefully constructed. How invitations arrived later than before, sometimes as afterthoughts. She did not complain. She adjusted. She always had.

Sanjay watched these changes from the edges. He was old enough to observe but not yet confident enough to question. He saw how his father continued to behave as if nothing had altered, how he maintained the same discipline, the same reliability. That consistency, once admired, now unsettled those who had grown comfortable depending on him without acknowledging it.

Envy did not arrive as jealousy. It arrived as irritation.

His father's capability had once protected everyone. Now it reminded them of their own dependence. The marriage gave that irritation a justification. It allowed resentment to be expressed indirectly, safely, under the language of tradition and concern.

They began to speak of family values. Of how things had been done earlier. Of how decisions should involve elders. Of how independence changed people.

The words were vague enough to deny accusation, specific enough to wound.

In meetings, Sanjay's father found himself interrupted more often. His suggestions were received politely and then reframed by others. Work he had completed years earlier was discussed as collective effort. Credit redistributed quietly, without challenge.

The atmosphere thickened.

Sanjay remembered an afternoon when his father returned home earlier than usual. He placed his bag down carefully and sat without removing his shoes. His mother noticed immediately. She asked nothing. She went to the kitchen and returned with water, setting the glass near him without sound.

That evening, they ate in silence.

Later that night, Sanjay stood in the doorway and watched his father sort through papers that did not require sorting. He straightened edges, rearranged files, aligned corners. The work was unnecessary. The control was not.

The next weeks carried this same weight. Nothing dramatic occurred. Instead, everything became slightly heavier. The joint family house felt colder, though the season had not changed. Conversations ended sooner. Decisions arrived already made.

When property discussions began formally, they were framed as inevitable. Practical. Necessary. The family had grown. Division would prevent future disputes. It was spoken of as wisdom.

Sanjay's father listened. He did not protest. He did not raise his voice. He believed that fairness, once documented, would settle everything.

The meetings took place in large rooms with windows that let in too much light. The sun fell harshly on tables where documents were spread. Advocates arrived with files that smelled of ink and time. Measurements were discussed. Boundaries drawn.

In those rooms, Sanjay watched the language of equality being used to formalize inequality. He did not yet have the vocabulary for it, but the sensation lodged somewhere permanent.

His father's share was discussed last.

What he received was presented as reasonable. Adequate. Balanced. A few acres of agricultural land that required explanation, defense, and eventually litigation to secure. The rest moved elsewhere with ease, absorbed into names that did not need to justify themselves.

The discussions ended without raised voices. Smiles were exchanged. Tea was served. The family congratulated itself on maturity.

That night, the weather changed.

It was not sudden. There was no storm. Just a shift in air pressure that made breathing feel deliberate. The joint family house closed in on itself. Invitations stopped arriving altogether. His mother was mentioned rarely, and when she was, it was with a careful distance that suggested obligation rather than affection.

Rumours began their quiet work.

They did not take form immediately. They arrived in fragments. Someone wondered aloud whether love marriages created instability. Someone recalled that things had been peaceful earlier. Someone mentioned influence, control, deviation.

No one accused directly. They did not need to. The repetition was enough.

Sanjay noticed how his father stopped attending certain gatherings. How he declined visits that once felt routine. How his mother's health began to fluctuate, her body reacting to pressures her voice refused to name.

The court cases followed.

The buildings were impersonal, constructed to discourage emotion. Benches bore the marks of generations who had waited without resolution. Sanjay accompanied his father often, sitting beside him, absorbing the procedural language that reduced family to claims and counterclaims.

The land itself remained silent. Fields did not care who stood on them. They yielded only to labour and rain.

When the judgment finally arrived, it was precise. It acknowledged his father's right to a limited portion. It denied the rest without commentary. Winning required relief rather than celebration.

The house they built afterward stood on its own plot, away from shared walls and shared stories. It rose slowly, financed through loans that measured time differently. Each installment marked progress. Each receipt confirmed survival.

The house smelled of cement and fresh paint. It did not carry ancestral echoes. It carried intention.

Sanjay's mother moved through its rooms carefully, placing furniture with restraint. She did not try to recreate what had been lost. She adapted. She always had.

The joint family's reaction was polite distance. They visited once. Complimented the construction. Asked about loans. Left without promise of return.

In the following months, the rumours grew clearer. Stories hardened. His mother's character was not attacked outright, but her influence was framed as excessive. Her presence became explanation for every inconvenience.

Sanjay heard these things indirectly. A neighbour's comment. A relative's hesitation. A phrase repeated with minor variation.

He began spending more time alone.

In the bathroom mirror, late at night, he studied his face as if it might reveal something he had missed. He spoke quietly, carefully, as if words themselves carried risk.

They are changing the story, he said.

The mirror returned his gaze without distortion.

He stood there longer than necessary, measuring the weight of that realization. Outside, the house settled into its new rhythm. Inside, something hardened, slowly, deliberately, learning the shape of endurance.

The weather after the wedding did not improve. It stabilized.

And that stability, he would later understand, was not peace. It was preparation.

Chapter Three

Land That Had to Be Won

The first time Sanjay entered the court complex with his father, the building appeared unfinished, though it had stood there for decades. Paint peeled unevenly from pillars. Notices were pasted one over another, old dates half-visible beneath newer ink. People moved through corridors with expressions that had learned patience by force. No one looked surprised to be there. No one expected resolution to arrive easily.

They reached early, as his father always did. Habit demanded it. He preferred to sit before the benches filled, before voices layered themselves into noise. The wooden seats were cold in the morning, their surfaces polished smooth by years of waiting bodies. Sanjay sat beside him, feet not quite touching the floor, watching advocates arrive with bulging files held close to their chests as if shielding something alive.

The case did not begin on time. It rarely did. Names were called out of order. Adjournments were announced casually, as if postponement were a neutral outcome. His father listened without visible reaction. He had learned long ago that irritation wasted energy better saved for documentation.

When their matter was finally mentioned, the language shifted. Family became parties. Years became dates. Labour became entitlement. The advocate spoke efficiently, referring to records that bore his father's handwriting from a time when he had still been trusted to manage them. Sanjay noticed that detail immediately, though no one else remarked upon it. The irony sat quietly between them.

Outside, the sun climbed higher. The courtyard filled with heat and impatience. People gathered in clusters, discussing cases with restrained urgency. His father stood slightly apart, reading through copies, making notes in the margins, preparing for questions that might or might not come. He did not speak about fairness. He spoke about proof.

The land in question lay on the outskirts of town, fields bordered by uneven fences and trees that offered inconsistent shade. Sanjay visited it once with his father, long before the judgment. They walked the boundary slowly, stopping where markers had shifted over time. The soil was dry, cracked in places, fertile in others. It did not look like inheritance. It looked like work.

This land had never been sentimental. It had not been spoken of as legacy or pride. It existed because records said it existed, because someone had decided it would be measured and divided. Others had accepted their portions without resistance. His father's share required contest.

The court hearings stretched across months. Dates shifted. Documents were requested again. Each visit followed the same pattern. Early arrival. Waiting. Brief exchanges heavy with consequence. Departure without certainty.

Sanjay learned the rhythm of it quickly. He learned where to sit, when to speak, when to remain silent. He observed how his father carried himself, neither pleading nor aggressive. He trusted procedure, even when it tested him.

At home, his mother's health began to falter more often. Some days she moved through the house with ease, preparing meals, arranging shelves, maintaining a routine that refused to acknowledge strain. Other days she rested longer, her body withdrawing from effort without explanation. She did not speak of rumours. She did not speak of court. She asked only whether they had eaten.

The house smelled of cement and new wood. It was clean, orderly, unburdened by shared history. Yet it felt watched, as if the absence of joint walls made it more exposed rather than less. Neighbours observed quietly. Conversations were polite. Curiosity lingered.

The judgment arrived without ceremony.

They were seated on the same bench when the clerk read it out, voice flat, uninvested. His father's right to a limited portion of land was acknowledged. The rest was dismissed. No commentary followed. The words settled into the room and waited to be understood.

Outside, his father folded the paper carefully and placed it in his bag. He did not smile. He did not sigh. Relief did not announce itself. They walked back through the courtyard in silence, passing others whose faces carried different versions of the same fatigue.

Winning did not restore anything that had been lost. It secured only what remained possible.

The land was registered finally in his father's name. Boundaries were confirmed. Markers fixed. The fields lay unchanged, indifferent to resolution. Sanjay accompanied him again, watching as officials measured and signed. The process was efficient now, procedural, stripped of argument. What had been contested had become fact.

The loans for the house continued.

Every month, payments were made on time. Receipts were stored carefully. The discipline of repayment shaped the household. Purchases were considered. Expenses tracked. Nothing was wasted. The house grew gradually more complete, furniture added when necessary, walls adorned minimally.

The joint family visited once after the judgment. They arrived in the afternoon, inspected the rooms, commented on ventilation and layout. Compliments were offered without warmth. Questions were asked about finances. The visit ended quickly. No return date was suggested.

After they left, the house felt larger, emptier.

Rumours grew bolder. The language shifted from suggestion to certainty. Stories repeated themselves with confidence earned through repetition. His mother's name circulated in conversations she never entered. Her influence was discussed as fact. Her intentions assumed.

Sanjay overheard fragments in markets, at bus stops, during visits to offices. He learned how easily narratives detached from truth and attached themselves to convenience. He did not respond. He recorded.

Late at night, he stood before the mirror again. The bathroom light cast a pale glow, flattening features, removing shadow. He looked at himself as if checking alignment.

They made us prove what others received, he said.

The mirror remained neutral.

He continued, quieter now. They turned responsibility into suspicion.

The words felt heavier than before. They did not demand resolution. They demanded endurance.

In the days that followed, his father returned to routine. Retirement approached. Files reduced. Mornings grew quieter. He still woke early, still read newspapers thoroughly, still marked articles with a pen he had used for years. He did not speak of the court again.

Sanjay began to understand that some battles did not end when judgments were delivered. They ended only when memory was allowed to rest. He did not intend to grant that rest easily.

The land lay beyond town, fields stretching under open sky. The house stood separate, financed, contained. The joint family house remained occupied by those who had benefited from its division. Life continued.

In the mirror, Sanjay watched his own reflection age slightly with understanding. The pain he carried did not demand expression. It demanded placement. He was learning where to put it, how to carry it without distortion, how to let it shape him without revealing itself.

The land had been won. Something else had been lost. He would not name it yet.

Naming, he understood, came later.

Chapter Four

What Rumours Sound Like

Rumours did not arrive as voices raised in accusation. They came as adjustments. As pauses that lengthened just enough to invite interpretation. As sentences that stopped short of conclusion and left space for agreement. Sanjay learned this gradually, the way one learns the sound of an approaching train before it becomes visible.

The first time he noticed it clearly was during a family gathering that had no stated purpose. An uncle had called and said everyone should meet, that it had been a while, that there was no reason except togetherness. The joint family house filled slowly that evening, chairs scraped across stone floors, ceiling fans turning with inconsistent rhythm. Plates were arranged, tea was poured, and conversation drifted across familiar ground before settling into quieter territory.

Sanjay sat near the doorway, a position he had learned offered both presence and distance. From there, he watched how his mother's name entered the room without her entering it herself. Someone mentioned how things had been simpler earlier. Someone else responded that times changed, that influences changed people. No one said her name. No one needed to.

His father listened, eyes steady, hands resting on his knees. He did not interrupt. He did not defend. Silence, he believed, still carried dignity. Sanjay noticed how that silence was no longer interpreted as strength. It was now read as avoidance.

After that evening, the gatherings became rarer. When they did occur, his parents were informed later than others. Invitations arrived incomplete, missing details, framed as afterthoughts. The joint family house, once familiar, began to feel foreign. Its rooms retained memory but withheld welcome.

Rumours matured through repetition. Each telling sharpened them. What began as suggestion solidified into assumed knowledge. Sanjay heard them in fragments. At a neighbour's house where tea cooled untouched. At a shop where someone lowered their voice unnecessarily. At a bus stop where a sentence trailed off as he approached.

He learned how people spoke differently when they believed they were being careful. Concern dressed itself as caution. Sympathy disguised itself as judgment. His mother's choices were framed as ambition. Her quietness was reinterpreted as calculation. Her illness, when mentioned, became convenient proof of imbalance.

His mother herself remained largely unaware of the full extent. She sensed the distance, felt the withdrawal, but did not collect evidence. She had grown up understanding that survival sometimes required not naming everything that hurt. When comments reached her directly, she absorbed them without reply. She adjusted her routines, reduced her visits, avoided unnecessary exposure.

At home, she moved through rooms with careful efficiency. Mornings were spent preparing meals, arranging medicine, maintaining a rhythm that refused to acknowledge intrusion. Some days her body resisted effort. Pain arrived without warning, settled into joints and breath. She rested when necessary, then returned to work without complaint.

Sanjay watched her closely. He learned how dignity survived through restraint. He also learned how restraint invited misinterpretation.

His father remained disciplined. Retirement had narrowed his external obligations but not his habits. He woke early, read thoroughly, marked margins. He took notes on matters that no longer required his attention. It was as if his mind refused to release the role it had been trained to play.

The rumours did not accuse him directly either. They questioned his judgment. His priorities. His loyalty to tradition. They spoke of influence again, of how marriage altered men, of how responsibilities shifted when personal interests intervened.

The cruelty lay in the tone. Nothing was stated with certainty. That would have required proof. Instead, doubt was introduced gently, allowed to grow in others' minds without resistance.

Sanjay experienced it most sharply in moments of absence. When he was not present, stories expanded. When he entered rooms, conversations adjusted. People became careful, overly polite, as if guarding against something unnamed.

He did not confront anyone. Confrontation, he sensed, would legitimize the narrative. It would invite defense, argument, alignment. Silence denied them that structure.

Instead, he listened.

He learned who repeated what. He noticed patterns. He observed how some relatives embellished while others merely nodded. He distinguished between those who believed and those who found belief convenient.

The joint family house continued to host events without them. Photos circulated later, glimpses of gatherings they were not part of. Sanjay saw these images with detachment. Exclusion, once recognized, lost some of its sting.

At night, the mirror became his confidant. The bathroom was small, its light harsh, its walls unadorned. Steam from earlier use clouded the glass until he wiped it clear with his palm. He studied his reflection carefully, as if checking for signs others claimed to see.

They are teaching each other how to say it, he said quietly.

The mirror held his gaze.

They say it without saying it.

He paused, considering the weight of those words. Rumours, he understood now, were not about truth. They were about repetition. They required no evidence, only consensus.

In the days that followed, he noticed how the rumours affected practical matters. His father's suggestions in shared concerns were no longer sought. When land-related issues arose in extended family contexts, others handled them poorly rather than consult him. Mistakes were made. Losses occurred. No one acknowledged the connection.

The family's narrative had shifted too far to allow correction.

Sanjay felt the accumulation of these moments not as anger but as pressure. It settled into his body, into his posture, into the way he listened. He became quieter, more observant. He spoke only when necessary, choosing words that could not be easily reinterpreted.

His mother's health fluctuated more visibly now. Doctors' visits became frequent. Diagnoses were discussed in clinical terms that failed to capture fatigue and hurt. Sanjay accompanied her often, sitting in waiting rooms that smelled of disinfectant and impatience. He watched how she answered questions carefully, minimizing discomfort, refusing drama.

Outside those rooms, he noticed how people spoke of her absence from family functions. They framed it as withdrawal, as avoidance, as evidence of the very narratives they had created.

The cruelty was efficient.

Sanjay began to understand that rumours did not need constant maintenance. Once established, they sustained themselves. Each retelling reinforced belief. Each silence confirmed it.

In the mirror, his voice grew steadier.

They will not stop, he said one night.

The mirror offered no reassurance.

He continued, almost clinically. They do not need to stop. They only need to believe they are right.

This realization did not bring relief. It brought clarity.

He stopped hoping for correction. He stopped expecting acknowledgment. Instead, he began storing memory differently. He recorded not events but patterns. He noted who benefited, who remained silent, who exaggerated, who merely followed.

The joint family's version of events grew polished. It was repeated at weddings, at funerals, at gatherings where his parents were absent. It became tradition, spoken with confidence earned through time.

Sanjay watched it solidify without interference.

The house remained orderly. The loans continued to be paid. Life proceeded with discipline. His parents aged quietly. Nothing external changed significantly.

Internally, something settled.

In the mirror, Sanjay no longer asked why. He did not question fairness. He acknowledged only permanence.

They will remember the lie, he said softly.

He waited, then added, with equal calm. I will remember who taught it.

The mirror reflected his face without alteration. The room remained silent. Outside, the neighbourhood prepared for sleep, unaware of the quiet education taking place within walls that did not announce their lessons.

Rumours had found their sound. Sanjay had learned to hear it clearly.

He did not respond.

He did not correct.

He remembered.

Chapter Five

Anaya

The college campus carried its own kind of weather, one that shifted not with seasons but with ambition. Buildings stood close together, their walls marked by notices layered one over another, announcements of seminars, placements, deadlines. Students moved through corridors with purpose that changed weekly, sometimes daily. Sanjay walked those paths without urgency. He was attentive rather than eager, observant rather than loud. It was there that he first noticed Anaya, not because she demanded attention, but because she absorbed it without effort.

She spoke with clarity. Her words arrived measured, confident, arranged as if she had rehearsed them privately before offering them aloud. When professors asked questions, she answered without hesitation. When discussions opened, she entered them naturally, drawing focus without appearing to seek it. Sanjay admired that composure. He admired the way she carried herself as if expectation were an ally rather than a burden.

At that time, his admiration was uncomplicated. He did not calculate advantage. He did not imagine leverage. He watched her from a distance that felt respectful, allowing appreciation to exist without demand. When conversations occurred, they were light, academic at first, then gradually personal. They spoke about coursework, about plans that remained vague enough to remain possible. She listened attentively, responded thoughtfully. Nothing suggested imbalance.

Sanjay was careful. He had grown up watching how narratives could shift when intentions were misread. He did not intrude. He waited. When admiration deepened into certainty, it did so quietly, without drama. He imagined her not as conquest or achievement but as alignment, someone who could stand beside him without distorting him.

At that stage of his life, he had no habits that required apology. He did not drink. He did not chase distractions. His routines were simple, disciplined, shaped by responsibility learned early. His interest in her was sincere, unadorned by strategy.

When he finally spoke of his feelings, he did so plainly. There was no theatrical confession, no dramatic appeal. He told her he admired her, that he respected her, that he wanted a future in which she was present not as an idea but as a partner. He expected clarity in return, even if that clarity took the form of refusal.

What he received instead was continuation.

She did not reject him outright. She did not accept him either. Her response was gentle, noncommittal, framed in consideration. She valued his presence. She appreciated his support. She was not ready, she said, for decisions that narrowed possibilities. There was still time. There was still growth ahead.

Sanjay accepted this at face value. He did not press. He believed that patience was a form of respect. He continued to admire her, to support her, to listen. Over time, his presence became consistent, dependable. He attended events where she spoke. He offered help when she asked. He celebrated her successes without inserting himself into them.

Years passed in this manner, measured by semesters and transitions. Sanjay noticed that her expectations expanded as opportunities presented themselves. Her ambitions sharpened. Her references shifted. She spoke of circles he did not belong to, of futures that required a different scale of association. He listened without resentment, still believing that alignment could adjust with time.

What changed was not her behaviour but his understanding of it.

He began to notice how his admiration energized her. How his attention functioned as reinforcement rather than connection. She enjoyed being admired. She enjoyed the certainty of his presence. It validated her without demanding reciprocity.

The realization did not arrive as betrayal. It arrived as clarity.

He understood that his emotion existed asymmetrically. What he offered carried weight for him alone. For her, it was additive, not essential. She did not manipulate him consciously. She did not promise what she did not intend to deliver. She simply allowed admiration to continue because it did not inconvenience her.

That understanding settled slowly. It did not wound immediately. It educated.

Sanjay did not confront her. Confrontation would have required accusation, and there was nothing to accuse. She had not deceived him. She had merely accepted what was given. Responsibility for imbalance rested with the giver.

He withdrew incrementally. Messages shortened. Visits reduced. Support remained polite but limited. He did not dramatize the change. He did not announce departure. He simply stopped offering what was not returned.

She noticed eventually. She asked whether something was wrong. He answered honestly but without appeal. He told her he had misunderstood the nature of their connection. He acknowledged his role in that misunderstanding. He did not ask for reconsideration.

Her response was mild surprise, followed by reassurance that he mattered, that his absence would be felt. It was sincere enough to soften but not enough to alter reality.

That conversation ended without resolution.

Sanjay walked away carrying neither anger nor hope. What he carried instead was a lesson.

He learned that admiration, when unbalanced, became currency for the admired. He learned that sincerity did not guarantee selection. He learned that emotional investment required regulation as much as financial or legal investment.

At home, life continued. His mother's health fluctuated. His father's routines remained unchanged. The house functioned with quiet discipline. Sanjay did not speak of Anaya to them. He did not frame the experience as loss. It did not feel like loss. It felt like closure without ceremony.

Late at night, the mirror received his words.

You mistook intensity for value, he said softly.

The mirror did not challenge him.

You offered without measuring.

He paused, studying his reflection. There was no bitterness there, only assessment.

That will not repeat.

From that point onward, Sanjay adjusted his relationship with emotion. He did not eliminate it. He constrained it. He learned to observe first, to measure response, to calculate symmetry before commitment. Emotion, he decided, was not dangerous. Unregulated emotion was.

He did not carry resentment toward Anaya. She remained part of his memory, not as antagonist but as instructor. She had shown him something essential without intending to.

In the days that followed, he redirected attention inward. He focused on studies, on systems, on understanding structures that rewarded control over sentiment. He watched how institutions functioned, how leverage accumulated quietly.

The campus remained the same. Anaya moved through it with confidence, her ambitions intact. Sanjay observed from a distance that felt appropriate now. He did not follow. He did not withdraw entirely. He adjusted.

In the mirror, weeks later, his voice was steadier.

Emotion is not currency, he said.

The mirror reflected agreement without confirmation.

That chapter of his life closed without spectacle. No one noticed its ending. No one needed to. What mattered was not how it concluded, but what it taught him about exchange, expectation, and the cost of offering more than one is prepared to lose.

He stepped away from the mirror and into routine, carrying the lesson carefully, already aware that it would not remain confined to love alone.

Chapter Six

The Day He Stopped Offering

Morning entered the house without ceremony. Light reached the floor in thin bands, touching edges of furniture before settling into corners. Sanjay woke before the alarm, as he had begun to do often, his body learning patterns before his mind acknowledged them. He lay still for a moment, listening to the house breathe. From the other room came the familiar sounds of his father moving quietly, opening a window, adjusting a chair. The routine remained intact. Something else had shifted.

He rose and walked to the bathroom. The mirror reflected a face that looked unchanged, though he knew it was not. He studied it carefully, the way one studies a document for discrepancies. No anger showed itself. No disappointment. Only recognition.

You are not owed balance, he said softly.

The words did not comfort him. They clarified.

The day proceeded normally. He attended classes, listened, took notes. Around him, conversations rose and fell, filled with ambition and anxiety. Students spoke of opportunities, of placements, of futures shaped by names and networks. Sanjay listened without urgency. He had begun noticing how often people spoke in anticipation rather than intent.

When he saw Anaya that day, it was in passing. She walked with friends, her posture confident, her laughter easy. She acknowledged him with a nod, a smile that held familiarity without invitation. It did not wound him. It confirmed what he already knew.

He did not follow. He did not linger. He continued walking, aware of the moment but not arrested by it.

That afternoon, he sat alone in the library, a place that suited his emerging temperament. The air smelled of paper and dust. Silence carried weight there, respected by those who entered. He opened a book on management systems, reading not for knowledge alone but for structure. He found comfort in frameworks that explained human behavior through processes rather than emotion.

He began to see patterns everywhere. How effort was rewarded only when visible. How sincerity without leverage became expendable. How systems absorbed individuals and returned outcomes without sentiment.

The realization did not embitter him. It disciplined him.

At home, his mother rested longer that evening. Her illness arrived quietly, settled into her joints, slowed her movements. He prepared dinner without comment, arranging plates with care. She thanked him, smiled, asked about his day. He answered briefly. She did not press. They had learned how to communicate without intrusion.

Later, as the house grew quiet, he returned to the mirror. The light cast a steady glow. He did not rush this time. He allowed the silence to settle before speaking.

You offered without measuring return, he said.

The mirror reflected his stillness.

That was the mistake.

He waited, then added, with equal calm. It will not repeat.

This was not a vow. It was a correction.

From that day onward, Sanjay adjusted how he engaged with the world. He did not withdraw entirely. Withdrawal invited speculation. Instead, he regulated. He gave attention sparingly. He listened more than he spoke. When he spoke, he chose words that could not be easily repurposed.

In conversations, he noticed how people responded to limits. Some respected them instinctively. Others tested them, pushing gently, expecting accommodation. He learned who required boundaries and who required distance.

He continued his studies with renewed focus. Management theories no longer felt abstract. They described realities he had already observed. He understood hierarchy not as cruelty but as inevitability. He learned that systems favored those who understood timing.

At the same time, the family narratives continued their quiet work. Rumours persisted, refined through repetition. His mother's absence from gatherings was framed as withdrawal. Her illness became a convenient explanation for imagined instability. Sanjay listened without reaction. He did not confront. He did not correct.

He stored everything.

Weeks passed. His routines solidified. He woke early, studied, assisted at home, maintained discipline. He did not seek distraction. He did not seek validation. Emotion was no longer something to be offered freely. It was to be evaluated, contained, deployed only when symmetry was assured.

Occasionally, he encountered Anaya again. Their exchanges remained polite, neutral. She spoke of plans, of opportunities. He listened without investment. She noticed the change eventually. She asked whether he was distant. He answered honestly, without accusation. He told her he had adjusted his expectations.

She seemed surprised, perhaps mildly disappointed. She said she valued his presence. He acknowledged that. He did not resume offering it.

That conversation ended without consequence.

At night, the mirror received fewer words. He no longer needed to explain his understanding. It had settled into him, becoming part of his posture, his listening, his silence.

Emotion had been reclassified.

It was no longer currency. It was no longer proof. It was a resource that required regulation.

He turned off the light and returned to his room. Outside, the neighborhood slept. Inside, something fundamental had concluded without announcement.

The day he stopped offering did not feel dramatic. It felt necessary.

And necessity, he understood, was the only justification that lasted.

Chapter Seven

Records Do Not Lie

The registration office opened at ten but began functioning earlier, not officially, not visibly, but in the way systems always did. Clerks arrived with newspapers folded under their arms, tea cups balanced carefully, keys jingling as doors were unlocked with practiced indifference. By the time the shutters rose, files already waited on desks, stacked unevenly, their weight measured not in pages but in years.

Sanjay arrived before the rush. He had learned that timing mattered as much as knowledge. Mornings were quieter. People were less defensive before fatigue arrived. He stood near the entrance, observing how others approached the building. Some came anxious, clutching documents as if afraid they might escape. Others walked in confidently, already rehearsing arguments meant to compensate for weak records.

He did not belong to either category.

When his turn came, he placed his papers on the counter without hurry. The clerk glanced at them briefly, then looked up with mild irritation, accustomed to correcting mistakes rather than confirming accuracy. Sanjay waited without explanation. Silence unsettled people who expected justification.

The clerk returned to the documents, slower this time. Pages were turned. Dates checked. Signatures traced with a finger that paused only once. He cleared his throat, a sound that suggested surprise he did not wish to display.

"These are complete," he said finally.

Sanjay nodded. He thanked him and stepped aside, making room for the next person whose documents would not be.

That moment did not feel significant. It felt correct.

Over the following months, Sanjay began appearing in offices like this with increasing frequency. He did not announce himself as a consultant. He did not claim expertise. He accompanied people who needed assistance, standing slightly behind them, offering clarification only when confusion threatened to derail proceedings. He knew where records failed, where boundaries blurred, where assumptions replaced documentation.

People noticed.

Not because he spoke loudly or asserted authority, but because problems ended when he was involved. Files moved. Disputes shortened. Errors were corrected before becoming liabilities. In places where inefficiency was expected, his presence felt disruptive in a way that could not be easily resisted.

He learned to read offices the way others read faces. He recognized which clerks valued procedure and which valued leverage. He adapted accordingly. He did not offer favors. He did not request exceptions. He spoke in the language of compliance, which paradoxically gave him more freedom than negotiation ever could.

At home, his mother's illness continued its quiet unpredictability. Some mornings she rose with ease, preparing breakfast, humming softly as she moved between rooms. Other mornings she remained seated longer, her breath measured, her body refusing momentum. Sanjay adjusted without comment. He took over tasks, managed appointments, accompanied her to hospitals where corridors smelled of disinfectant and resignation.

In waiting rooms, he observed systems under strain. Patients waited not only for doctors but for acknowledgment. Nurses moved efficiently, compassion rationed by workload. Sanjay noted how authority functioned differently here, how vulnerability rearranged hierarchies temporarily. He spoke respectfully, clearly, without urgency. It earned him cooperation without familiarity.

His father watched these developments with quiet pride he did not articulate. Retirement had reduced his formal responsibilities, but habit remained. He read newspapers thoroughly, marked articles concerning land, law, administration. Sometimes he asked Sanjay questions, phrased casually, about procedures, about changes in regulation. Sanjay answered precisely, without embellishment.

In the evenings, they sat together in the front room, television murmuring without engagement. The house remained orderly, its routines predictable. Outside, the neighborhood shifted subtly. People noticed Sanjay's comings and goings. They began asking questions indirectly.

Someone mentioned a boundary issue. Someone else asked about inheritance documentation. Sanjay responded cautiously at first, clarifying rather than advising. Over time, those clarifications became solutions.

He did not advertise. He did not distribute cards. His reputation traveled through conclusion rather than promise.

The mirror witnessed these changes in tone rather than content. At night, Sanjay stood before it briefly, assessing not pain now but alignment. He spoke less. The questions had been answered already. What remained was execution.

Records do not lie, he said once, softly.

The mirror held his reflection steady.

People do.

The sentence did not accuse. It categorized.

As his involvement increased, he encountered resistance. Some officials bristled at his precision. Others resented his refusal to engage in informal arrangements. A few tested him, delaying processes unnecessarily, expecting concession. He responded with patience that outlasted obstruction. He documented interactions. He followed up methodically. He allowed inefficiency to expose itself.

Eventually, those obstacles softened. Not out of respect, but out of exhaustion.

The disputes he resolved were not dramatic. They involved missing signatures, overlapping claims, outdated records. Each resolution reinforced a pattern. When Sanjay handled it, the matter concluded. People began seeking him out deliberately, preferring quiet certainty over aggressive advocacy.

He learned where influence accumulated. Not in overt displays, but in consistency. Not in alliances, but in reliability.

At the same time, family narratives continued to circulate. Rumours about his mother persisted, now reinforced by distance and absence. Sanjay noticed how those stories lost urgency outside the family context. In offices, among officials, among people who interacted with him professionally, those rumours held no weight. Documentation mattered more.

That realization settled deeply.

Reputation, he understood, was portable only when backed by systems. Narrative could destroy character within closed circles. It failed against records.

He began to see a division emerging between two worlds. One governed by memory and rumor. The other governed by documentation and procedure. He felt increasingly aligned with the latter.

This alignment did not erase pain. It repositioned it.

At night, the mirror received fewer confessions. Sanjay no longer needed to articulate what he carried. The pain had been archived, placed where it could be accessed without spilling.

His days grew structured. Mornings at offices. Afternoons assisting clients. Evenings at home. He maintained discipline, avoiding excess. Emotion remained regulated. His interactions were courteous, restrained, purposeful.

People began introducing him to others as someone who understood land matters well. He corrected them gently, saying he understood processes. The distinction mattered.

As weeks turned into months, the number of matters he handled increased. He did not charge initially. He learned. He observed outcomes. When he began charging, it was modest, justified by resolution rather than time spent.

Officials recognized his name. Not with enthusiasm, but with caution. Files bearing his handwriting were checked carefully. Errors were avoided preemptively. He noticed the change without comment.

In the mirror, one night, he acknowledged it quietly.

They are careful now.

The mirror reflected neither approval nor warning.

Care, he knew, preceded fear.

He turned away from the glass and returned to routine, aware that he was building something intangible, something that did not announce itself but would eventually weigh on those who underestimated it.

Records did not lie.

And he was learning how to make them speak.

Chapter Eight

The Restaurant on the Corner

The restaurant stood at the edge of a junction that never quite slept. Traffic slowed there not because of signals but because of habit. Drivers knew the curve instinctively, eased their vehicles without thinking, allowed the road to gather itself before continuing. Sanjay chose the location deliberately. Visibility mattered, but prominence did not. He wanted the place to be known without being announced.

The building was modest, its frontage plain, the signboard unremarkable. No dramatic colors, no slogans promising excess. Inside, the space was clean and restrained. Tables were arranged with enough distance to allow conversation without intrusion. The kitchen was visible through a glass partition, not as spectacle but as assurance. Nothing was hidden. Nothing needed to be.

He did not open the restaurant as a passion project. Food was not sentiment for him. It was structure. Routine. Supply chains. Staff management. Cash flow that could be observed daily. A business that required consistency more than charisma.

The first weeks were slow. Customers arrived cautiously, surveyed the space, assessed prices. Some came once and did not return. Others returned quietly, bringing family, then colleagues. Sanjay spent long hours there, not behind the counter but among tables, observing how people behaved in spaces they believed were neutral.

He learned how men spoke when they were not in offices. How authority softened when removed from desks. How grievances surfaced over meals, unguarded. Property disputes were mentioned casually. Boundary issues laughed off, then revisited seriously. Names surfaced. Locations. Disagreements framed as inconveniences rather than threats.

Sanjay listened without appearing to.

He moved through the restaurant with calm familiarity, greeting customers without intimacy, resolving issues without apology. Staff learned quickly that efficiency mattered. Orders were expected to be accurate. Delays were corrected without shouting. Mistakes were addressed privately. Respect was non-negotiable.

The restaurant developed a rhythm. Mornings were quieter, filled with regulars who preferred familiarity. Afternoons brought officials from nearby offices, eating quickly, discussing files they would return to later. Evenings belonged to families, conversations overlapping, laughter contained.

Sanjay noticed how his presence influenced atmosphere. When he was there, people behaved differently. Not deferentially, but carefully. He did not impose rules. He embodied them.

At home, his mother's health remained variable. Some days she visited the restaurant briefly, sitting at a corner table, observing without comment. Staff treated her with respect, sensing importance without explanation. She did not interfere. She smiled occasionally, her presence grounding without instruction.

His father visited less often. He preferred the house, the quiet routines of retirement. When he did come, he sat near the entrance, watching customers enter and leave. He asked few questions. Pride, when it appeared, did so in posture rather than words.

The neighborhood responded gradually. The restaurant became a reference point. Directions were given using it. Meetings were scheduled around it. It integrated itself into daily life without demanding recognition.

Sanjay paid attention to this integration. Familiarity, he understood, was a form of protection. When a place became ordinary, it became trusted.

One afternoon, a minor dispute occurred. A customer complained about a bill, claiming an item had been added incorrectly. The staff hesitated, uncertain how to respond. Sanjay approached calmly, reviewed the bill, checked the order slip, confirmed the error. He apologized briefly, corrected the amount, and offered no justification beyond acknowledgment.

The customer left satisfied, surprised more by the efficiency than the concession.

Others noticed.

Incidents like this accumulated. Sanjay resolved them quietly, without escalating emotion. Over time, customers began deferring to his judgment instinctively. When disagreements arose between patrons, he mediated with minimal words. His voice carried authority because it never competed.

Outside the restaurant, his work in property matters continued. People he met there began approaching him privately, asking questions about land records, about inheritance documentation. He listened, offered guidance, suggested steps. He did not solicit business. He allowed it to find him.

The restaurant functioned as a social cross-section. Officials, traders, families, workers. Sanjay observed how narratives shifted across contexts. Stories that sounded convincing at dining tables collapsed when placed beside records. He noted the contrast carefully.

At night, when the restaurant closed, he stayed back to review accounts. Cash was counted precisely. Expenses tracked. Staff payments recorded. He insisted on transparency. Not because he feared accusation, but because he understood how quickly narratives formed in the absence of clarity.

The mirror appeared again in his routine, though less frequently. When it did, the conversations were brief.

Visibility without exposure, he said once.

The mirror reflected agreement without expression.

The restaurant did not make him wealthy quickly. It made him present. It anchored him in public life without making him vulnerable to gossip. People saw him daily, behaving consistently. That consistency softened the edges of the rumours circulating within family spaces. Outside those circles, his mother's name carried no weight. His actions defined him more clearly than stories ever could.

He began noticing a shift in how officials interacted with him. Casual conversations grew cautious. Questions were framed carefully. When he appeared in offices regarding property matters, recognition flickered briefly before neutrality resumed. His reputation traveled ahead of him now, not loudly, but reliably.

The restaurant became part of that reputation. A place that functioned smoothly, where issues were resolved without spectacle. People trusted spaces as much as individuals. He understood that instinctively.

One evening, during a power outage, the restaurant fell briefly into darkness. Conversations paused. Phones lit tables with pale screens. Staff waited for instruction. Sanjay moved calmly, arranging candles stored for such events, instructing staff to reassure customers, coordinating without urgency. Within minutes, the atmosphere stabilized.

When power returned, customers resumed eating as if nothing had occurred.

That moment mattered more than it appeared. In uncertainty, people watched how leadership manifested. Sanjay did not dramatize disruption. He absorbed it.

At home later that night, he stood before the mirror longer than usual. The house was quiet. His mother slept. His father read in the other room.

You are learning scale, he said to his reflection.

The mirror did not disagree.

Scale, he knew, determined outcome. Small disruptions revealed large weaknesses. Large plans failed because of neglected details. The restaurant taught him how to manage both simultaneously.

As months passed, the restaurant's finances stabilized. Profit arrived steadily, without spikes. Sanjay reinvested cautiously, upgrading equipment, training staff. He avoided expansion for its own sake. Growth, he believed, should follow readiness.

The rumours within the family persisted, but their reach felt increasingly confined. Sanjay sensed a separation forming between the world he inhabited publicly and the one that continued narrating his parents privately. That division did not distress him. It clarified priorities.

In the mirror, he no longer spoke of pain. He spoke of placement.

Everything has its place, he said softly.

The mirror held his gaze.

Including memory.

He turned off the light and left the bathroom. Outside, the junction continued its slow rhythm. Vehicles passed, slowed, continued. The restaurant slept behind its shutter, prepared for the next day without anticipation or anxiety.

Sanjay understood that this was how influence accumulated. Quietly. Repetitively. Without confession.

And he continued.

Chapter Nine

Concrete and Names

The first construction site Sanjay visited as a collaborator did not look impressive. It was a cleared plot with uneven ground, marked by white chalk lines that tried to impose order on soil that resisted it. A temporary shed stood at one corner, its tin roof rattling slightly in the wind. The smell of wet earth mixed with cement dust lingered in the air, sharp and metallic.

The partners arrived in sequence, some confident, some cautious. They spoke about square footage, budgets, timelines. Their voices carried the optimism of men who believed growth itself justified risk. Sanjay listened more than he spoke. He had learned that early enthusiasm often hid later panic.

He walked the site slowly, stepping carefully over rebar and debris, visualizing structures not as images but as processes. Foundations first. Permissions next. Materials. Labour. Compliance. He asked questions that were not about ambition but about endurance. What delays had been factored in. Which approvals were pending. Who was responsible when timelines slipped.

Some partners grew impatient. Others grew attentive.

Construction, he understood, revealed character faster than conversation. Corners tempted men. Shortcuts whispered constantly. Those who resisted them earned longevity. Those who indulged them built faster and collapsed earlier.

The first project progressed steadily. There were delays, but they were managed. Costs increased slightly, but transparency prevented suspicion. When issues arose, Sanjay addressed them directly, documenting decisions, clarifying responsibilities. He did not assign blame. He assigned process.

Officials visited the site occasionally. They walked through with practiced disinterest, checking measurements, asking routine questions. Sanjay answered clearly, without hesitation. Documents were produced immediately. No scrambling. No apologies.

The inspections ended quickly.

As the building rose, so did attention. Not excitement, but recognition. The name associated with the project appeared in conversations without emphasis.

People began asking who had structured it so cleanly. The answer varied, depending on who spoke. Sanjay did not correct them.

Another project followed, slightly larger. Then another. Each one involved collaboration rather than control. He avoided sole ownership deliberately. Shared risk kept everyone careful.

In offices, his presence was noted now. Clerks recognized him. Files moved with slightly more urgency. Questions were phrased more precisely. When delays occurred, explanations were offered without demand.

This was the point where the city entered his life as an entity rather than a backdrop.

In Mysore, construction did not attract attention for its height or novelty. It attracted attention for its alignment. Old neighborhoods resisted disruption. Officials remembered precedents. Families remembered land histories. Growth occurred quietly, negotiated through layers of memory and restraint.

Sanjay navigated this landscape with instinctive caution. He did not attempt to accelerate what resisted speed. He respected boundaries that others tested. That respect returned to him as cooperation.

The restaurant continued its steady rhythm. The consultancy handled more complex disputes now. People spoke of him with confidence reserved for reliability rather than charisma.

At home, his mother's health remained fragile but stable. His father followed developments with quiet interest, reading about zoning changes, infrastructure plans. Sometimes he commented on how things had shifted since his own years in service. Sanjay listened, absorbing context without nostalgia.

The mirror reflected a man who had stopped measuring pain and started measuring consequence.

Names mattered now. Not his, but those associated with projects, approvals, responsibility. He understood that the city remembered names longer than intentions.

In Mysore, reputation moved slowly but settled permanently.

Sanjay continued building, aware that each structure added weight not just to the skyline, but to the ledger of trust he was compiling silently.

And trust, once established, would become something far more difficult to undo.

Chapter Ten

The Office That Listened

The consultancy office occupied a narrow stretch above a row of shops that sold electrical parts and stationery. Its staircase was steep, the steps worn smooth by years of use, the handrail polished by palms that had climbed without thinking. Sanjay chose the space because it did not invite attention. People who came there came deliberately. Accidental visitors did not climb those stairs.

Inside, the office was spare. A desk near the window, two chairs opposite it, a filing cabinet pushed against the wall. The window overlooked a street that carried constant movement without drama. Buses passed. Two-wheelers paused. Vendors negotiated space. Nothing lingered long enough to claim ownership of the view.

The office did not advertise expertise. There were no certificates on the walls, no framed degrees. Files occupied the shelves, arranged by category rather than chronology. Disputes, registrations, inheritances, constructions. Each file carried a story that had already exhausted someone.

People arrived cautiously at first. They spoke in lowered voices, as if the walls themselves might repeat what they heard. Sanjay listened without interruption, allowing narratives to unfold fully before addressing them. He asked questions that redirected attention from emotion to fact. Dates. Measurements. Records. Assumptions collapsed quickly under that scrutiny.

He did not promise outcomes. He outlined processes.

This disappointed some and reassured others. Those who sought miracles left early. Those who sought resolution stayed.

Over time, the office developed a reputation that did not rely on success alone. It relied on clarity. People left knowing what could not be done as clearly as what could. That certainty mattered.

Sanjay noticed how conflicts softened once uncertainty was removed. Families argued less when boundaries were defined. Partners negotiated differently when obligations were documented. Lies struggled to survive in rooms where records were central.

The office listened more than it spoke.

A man arrived one afternoon carrying a bundle of papers tied loosely with string. He spoke rapidly, his words overlapping, his frustration visible. He believed a cousin had cheated him in a land division. He wanted intervention, urgency, action. Sanjay waited until the narrative concluded, then untied the bundle and sorted the papers silently.

Minutes passed. The man shifted in his chair, uncomfortable with the pause.

"You were present when this was signed," Sanjay said finally, pointing to a document.

"Yes," the man replied. "But I did not understand."

Sanjay nodded. "Understanding is not required for validity."

The man stared at the paper, anger dissolving into resignation. The dispute ended there. Not because it was resolved emotionally, but because it had been clarified legally.

Others arrived with more complex matters. Properties built without approvals. Extensions added quietly. Titles transferred informally. Sanjay did not scold. He outlined risk. He explained consequence. People adjusted their positions accordingly.

Officials began recognizing the address. They did not visit often, but when they did, they were careful. The files there were orderly. Questions were answered directly. There were no surprises.

The office became a place where things were decided before becoming public problems.

At home, his mother's routines continued to fluctuate. Some days she rested longer, her breath shallow, her movements measured. Sanjay adjusted his schedule, ensuring she was never alone during difficult hours. He managed appointments, medications, documentation. Care, he understood, was also a system. It required attention, discipline, patience.

His father observed this with quiet acceptance. He had carried responsibility for years. Watching his son assume it without complaint felt like continuation rather than replacement.

In the evenings, Sanjay returned to the office to review files alone. The building settled into silence. Outside, the street quieted slightly, the day releasing its grip. He organized documents, updated notes, prepared for meetings that would require precision rather than persuasion.

The mirror appeared again in his routine, now located in the small washroom adjoining the office. The light there was harsher, the reflection less forgiving. He spoke to it briefly, efficiently.

Listen first, he said.

The mirror returned the instruction without emphasis.

Do not absorb what is not yours.

The words mattered more now. As his influence expanded, so did the weight of others' expectations. People began attributing outcomes to him, crediting him for resolutions that had been procedural rather than personal. He corrected them when necessary, redirecting attention to process. He avoided becoming indispensable. Dependency bred resentment.

The family rumours persisted, but their reach felt increasingly limited. Within the consultancy, within offices, within public interactions, those stories held no currency. Documentation erased gossip effectively.

Sanjay noticed how his mother's name was absent from conversations here. She existed only as his responsibility, not as narrative. That absence felt protective.

In Mysore, such separations mattered. The city remembered what was repeated consistently and forgot what lacked reinforcement. Sanjay understood this intuitively. He allowed one narrative to fade by refusing to participate in it, while strengthening another through visible action.

The consultancy began handling cases involving construction approvals, zoning adjustments, compliance issues. These required coordination across departments. Sanjay navigated them carefully, never pushing, never pleading. He presented complete files, anticipated objections, resolved them before they surfaced.

Officials grew accustomed to this efficiency. They did not like it. They respected it.

Police presence brushed against his work occasionally. Disputes escalated beyond paperwork, voices raised, threats implied. Sanjay addressed these moments calmly, reminding parties of consequence, documenting statements, ensuring neutrality. Officers observed without intervention. They recognized control when they saw it.

No one attempted to intimidate him. Intimidation required leverage. He offered none.

At night, the mirror conversations grew rarer. When they occurred, they focused not on pain but on calibration.

You are visible now, he said once.

The mirror reflected the truth without comment.

Visibility required restraint. He adjusted accordingly. He limited appearances. He delegated tasks. He maintained consistency.

The office continued listening.

One evening, as he locked the door and descended the staircase, Sanjay paused briefly on the landing. The street below carried its usual rhythm. Lights flickered on. Shops closed. The city settled.

He understood then that this phase of his life was not preparation alone. It was establishment. He was placing himself where narratives struggled to reach and records held authority.

He did not feel satisfaction. Satisfaction implied completion.

What he felt was alignment.

He continued down the stairs, keys steady in his hand, aware that every step taken quietly added weight to a future that would not need explanation.

Chapter Eleven

The Boundary

The villa stood at the end of a narrow lane that curved slightly before arriving at its gate, as if reluctant to reveal what lay beyond too quickly. A half-acre was enough space to feel separate without feeling isolated. The land sloped gently toward the back, bordered by an uneven line of trees that caught wind differently depending on season. The house itself was practical, single-storied, built for endurance rather than display. Windows faced inward toward the garden more than outward toward the road.

The dog had arrived years earlier, small then, uncertain, its ribs visible beneath fur that had not yet learned shine. Sanjay had not planned for it. Someone had mentioned a litter near a construction site, unwanted, left to manage survival on instinct alone. He had gone to look without intention, returned with responsibility.

The dog adapted quickly. It learned the rhythms of the house faster than any person ever could. It waited by the door at certain hours, followed predictable paths through rooms, recognized moods without instruction. It did not demand attention. It accepted presence as enough.

Sanjay fed it himself, morning and evening, the routine becoming as fixed as any other. He spoke to it rarely. Affection was expressed through consistency rather than touch. The dog slept near the doorway, alert even in rest, ears shifting at unfamiliar sounds.

Over time, the dog grew comfortable beyond the gate. It wandered along the lane, returned reliably. Neighbours noticed. Children called to it. Hands reached through the fence. The dog responded without hesitation. It did not understand exclusivity. It understood availability.

At first, Sanjay did not object. He observed. Observation had taught him patience. He watched how the dog's attention expanded, how it lingered longer near the neighbouring house, how it returned carrying the scent of other homes. The dog remained obedient, returned when called, slept where it always had.

Still, something shifted.

The boundary was no longer clear.

The neighbour was a man who spoke easily, laughed often, and believed familiarity was proof of goodness. He greeted Sanjay warmly, commented on the dog's friendliness, offered food casually, without malice. The dog accepted it without pause.

Sanjay acknowledged the greetings without warmth or hostility. He did not explain himself. He did not issue instruction. He observed the pattern repeating.

The dog began waiting near the fence during afternoons. Its body angled outward. Its attention pulled elsewhere. When Sanjay returned home, it greeted him as always, tail wagging, posture unchanged. Loyalty, it believed, could be distributed.

That assumption unsettled him more than defiance ever could.

He did not react immediately. Reaction would have been premature. He monitored the situation with the same restraint he applied to everything else. Days passed. Then weeks. The behaviour did not correct itself. The dog did not understand the problem because there was none from its perspective.

Sanjay understood then that affection, when unregulated, expanded indiscriminately.

One evening, as dusk settled unevenly across the garden, Sanjay stood near the gate and watched the dog sit by the fence, waiting. The neighbour's voice carried faintly from the adjacent house. The dog's ears tilted forward.

Sanjay called it once. The dog hesitated, then returned, obedient but reluctant. The hesitation lasted only a moment. That moment mattered.

Inside the house, his mother rested, her breathing shallow but steady. His father read in the front room, the television muted. The routines continued uninterrupted.

Later that night, Sanjay stood before the mirror longer than usual. The light exposed lines he had not noticed before, not from age but from concentration. He spoke without raising his voice.

Affection that spills outward becomes disorder.

The mirror did not resist the statement.

He slept little that night.

The decision, when it arrived, did not feel like anger. It felt like correction.

The next morning unfolded as any other. He fed the dog. He allowed it into the garden. He watched it move freely, trusting without hesitation. He completed his routines, spoke to his parents, left the house briefly for work.

When he returned, the lane was quiet. The neighbour's house stood open, voices drifting faintly. The dog was not visible.

Sanjay waited.

Minutes passed. Then more. He called once. The dog did not appear. He did not call again.

When the dog returned, its posture was relaxed, content, carrying the smell of elsewhere. It approached Sanjay with the same familiarity it always had.

Sanjay looked at it without expression.

He did not speak.

What followed was not dramatic. There was no raised voice, no struggle that announced itself beyond the garden. The act itself was quick, contained, performed with efficiency rather than emotion. There was no witness. There was no spectacle.

The garden returned to stillness.

Sanjay washed his hands carefully afterward, scrubbing longer than necessary, not from guilt but from habit. Cleanliness mattered. Order mattered.

Inside, his parents remained unaware. His mother slept. His father continued reading, turning pages at measured intervals.

The absence revealed itself gradually. The gate remained quiet. No footsteps followed. No presence waited.

His father noticed first.

"The dog hasn't come today," he said, casually, without concern.

Sanjay nodded. "It won't."

There was no follow-up question.

At night, the mirror reflected a face that had not changed. Sanjay studied it without expectation.

You cannot share what you cannot control, he said.

The mirror offered no comfort.

This was not cruelty, he understood. Cruelty required pleasure. This was enforcement.

The loss did not pain him in the way others might expect. Pain required attachment that assumed permanence. He had already learned that assumption was false.

What remained was clarity.

Boundaries, once breached, did not repair themselves. They required action.

The house adjusted quickly. Absence settled into routine. The garden remained orderly. The lane continued its rhythm.

Sanjay continued his work without interruption. The consultancy handled disputes. The restaurant functioned. Construction sites progressed. Reputation expanded.

Inside, something had concluded.

The dog had been a test he had not realized he was conducting. It had revealed what happened when affection was left unmanaged. He stored the lesson carefully, alongside others.

In the mirror, days later, he did not speak of it again.

Some corrections, once made, required no repetition.

The boundary held.

And nothing crossed it without consequence.

Chapter Twelve

What They Still Said About Her

Rumours did not grow louder with time. They grew steadier. They settled into conversation the way habits settled into bodies, unnoticed until interruption made them visible. Sanjay understood this now. He heard it in the tone people used when they spoke of his mother, the careful modulation that pretended sympathy while insisting on judgment.

It began with absence. She stopped attending gatherings that required stamina she no longer possessed. Her illness made travel difficult. Her breath shortened unpredictably. Some days she could move through rooms with measured ease, others she remained seated, conserving energy for tasks that mattered. Sanjay arranged her world accordingly. Appointments were scheduled precisely. Medicines were logged. Meals were adjusted. Nothing was left to improvisation.

Outside that house, the absence was interpreted.

People said she kept away deliberately. They said she preferred isolation. They said she had always been that way, even before the marriage. The words carried certainty that did not require proof. Each retelling added confidence. Each nod reinforced the story.

Sanjay heard fragments through intermediaries. A relative mentioned concern during a phone call that lingered longer than necessary. A neighbour repeated something she had heard elsewhere, adding a detail she could not source. A distant cousin asked casually whether his mother was comfortable being alone so often.

Sanjay answered politely. He did not explain. Explanation invited evaluation. He had learned that clarity was useful only in systems that respected it.

The family gatherings continued without them. Photos circulated afterward, sent without invitation, presented as courtesy. Faces smiled. Food crowded tables. Familiar walls held conversations that no longer paused when his parents were mentioned. In those rooms, the story had been settled.

They spoke of the marriage again. They revisited the beginning, reinterpreting intentions. They spoke of ambition, of influence, of disruption. They described his mother as a force that had altered his father's trajectory. They said he had changed after marriage, that responsibility had turned into control, that affection had turned into expectation.

Sanjay recognized the pattern. When people benefited from injustice, they explained it as necessity. When they benefited from cruelty, they explained it as consequence.

His father did not address these stories. He continued his routines, maintaining dignity through refusal to engage. He read, he wrote notes, he watched the world without commentary. Sometimes he paused longer at certain articles, those involving family disputes, land cases, matters that echoed his own history. He did not speak of parallels.

Sanjay noticed how this silence was now framed as guilt.

They said he had nothing to say because there was nothing to defend. They said silence was confirmation. They said if the accusations were false, he would respond.

Sanjay understood then that silence no longer functioned as protection. It functioned as permission.

The cruelty sharpened.

Someone remarked openly during a gathering that love marriages rarely ended well. Another added that such unions often disrupted family harmony. Someone else suggested that illness followed instability. No one mentioned names. No one needed to.

Sanjay's mother heard none of this directly. Her world had narrowed to the house, the hospital, occasional visitors who arrived with genuine concern rather than curiosity. She did not collect rumours. She sensed them only through the way others adjusted their behavior, through invitations that never came, through conversations that ended quickly.

One afternoon, she asked Sanjay whether the family was upset with her.

He paused before answering. The pause mattered.

"They speak," he said finally. "It doesn't change anything."

She looked at him for a moment longer than usual, then nodded. She did not ask what they said. She had learned long ago that knowledge sometimes increased pain without offering remedy.

Later that evening, Sanjay stood before the mirror. The light was steady, unforgiving. He did not rush his words.

They are still saying it, he said.

The mirror held his gaze.

They are saying it more confidently now.

Confidence, he understood, was not evidence. It was repetition.

The rumours began affecting practical matters. Invitations to family functions stopped entirely. Decisions regarding ancestral matters were communicated indirectly, after they had been finalized. His parents' names were omitted from discussions that once required their involvement. Exclusion became procedural.

In professional contexts, the rumours found no traction. Offices functioned on records. Consultants required clarity. Officials valued documentation. The narratives circulating within family spaces could not penetrate these systems. That separation offered protection, but it also sharpened contrast.

Sanjay saw clearly how stories functioned as weapons only within closed circles. Outside them, they dissolved.

This realization did not bring relief. It brought focus.

One evening, a distant relative visited unexpectedly. The conversation remained polite, superficial. Tea was served. Health was discussed. As the visit drew to a close, the relative hesitated, then spoke in a voice softened by pretense.

"You know," he said, "people talk. It might help if your mother came around more. Just to clear misunderstandings."

Sanjay listened without interruption.

"What misunderstandings," he asked.

The man smiled uncomfortably. "Nothing specific. Just… perceptions."

Sanjay nodded. "Perceptions belong to those who create them."

The man left shortly afterward, unsettled by the lack of argument.

That night, Sanjay did not sleep immediately. He replayed conversations, not to feel them again, but to trace their structure. The family's narrative was now complete. It no longer required maintenance. It would persist on its own.

He understood then that his revenge, if it ever arrived, would not be about property. Property had already been divided, contested, settled. It would not be about money. Money could not repair what had been damaged.

It would be about narrative.

They had taken a woman who wanted only family and turned her into explanation. They had taken a man who carried responsibility and turned him into suspect. They had done this quietly, patiently, without conscience.

Sanjay returned to the mirror and spoke with measured calm.

They made a story and lived inside it.

The mirror reflected his stillness.

They will die inside it too.

He did not mean death then. Not yet. He meant erasure. He meant exposure. He meant collapse of certainty.

In the days that followed, he adjusted his movements. He reduced contact with family spaces further. He focused on professional routines, on maintaining stability at home. His mother's health required more attention now. He ensured comfort, managed pain, maintained dignity.

He did not confront anyone. Confrontation would have required acknowledgment of authority he refused to grant.

The rumours continued.

Sanjay allowed them to.

He was no longer interested in stopping them. He was interested in understanding how they traveled, who repeated them most enthusiastically, who remained silent, who benefited.

The mirror witnessed fewer words now. The conversations had shifted from pain to placement.

Everything they say has a place, he said once.

The mirror did not question him.

He was no longer carrying the rumours. He was mapping them.

And maps, he knew, were meant to be used.

Chapter Thirteen

The Invitation

The idea arrived without urgency. It did not announce itself as revenge or strategy. It appeared the way solutions sometimes did, fully formed, as if it had been waiting for permission rather than invention. Sanjay recognized it not by excitement but by calm. Calm was how he identified decisions that would last.

The invitation required neutrality. That was its strength. It could not look like summons or reconciliation. It had to resemble inevitability, the kind that arrived wrapped in benefit rather than demand. He considered several forms and discarded them quietly. Family gatherings were too obvious. Religious occasions carried expectations he did not intend to fulfill. Legal meetings would attract scrutiny.

The college reunion suggested itself almost casually.

Time had passed enough for nostalgia to feel safe. Distance had softened rivalries, sharpened curiosity. People liked to return to beginnings when their present allowed them to. The reunion could be framed as opportunity, as networking, as shared memory. It could gather individuals without exposing intention.

He began with logistics.

A private luxury resort on the outskirts, removed enough to feel exclusive, accessible enough to feel reasonable. Not ostentatious, but carefully maintained. The kind of place where people behaved differently, conscious of surroundings that suggested importance without declaring it. He selected a venue that understood discretion as service.

Arrangements were made quietly. Contracts signed. Schedules coordinated. No shortcuts. No unnecessary communication. He preferred staff who listened without asking questions. Money facilitated that preference.

The guest list was assembled gradually. Old classmates. Familiar names. Some successful, some stalled, all curious. Invitations were sent formally, framed as professional reconnection rather than sentiment. The language was precise, neutral, inviting without pleading.

Responses arrived steadily.

People were interested. Some surprised. Some pleased. Some cautious. Sanjay noted each reaction without interpretation. Attendance mattered less than willingness.

He ensured his presence was felt without being emphasized. His name appeared on the invitation as organizer, consultant, collaborator. No titles that invited challenge. No descriptions that invited comparison.

Anaya's name appeared naturally on the list.

He did not hesitate when he added it. Hesitation would have suggested unresolved emotion. There was none. What remained was relevance.

He did not contact her directly. That would have implied intention. Instead, the invitation reached her the same way it reached others, through channels that suggested professionalism rather than memory. The influence of his current position did the rest. Attendance was advantageous. Absence was noticeable.

She responded after a delay that suggested consideration rather than indifference.

Yes, she wrote. Looking forward to reconnecting.

Sanjay read the message once and closed it.

At home, his mother's health required closer monitoring. Pain arrived more frequently now, settling into her joints, narrowing her breath. Sanjay adjusted schedules accordingly, ensuring she was never alone during difficult hours. He arranged medical visits, consulted specialists, maintained records. Care remained procedural. Emotion followed structure.

His father observed these preparations without inquiry. He had learned that Sanjay did not act without reason. He trusted outcome more than explanation.

The days leading up to the reunion unfolded without tension. Sanjay maintained routine. He visited offices. Oversaw construction matters. Checked restaurant accounts. The consultancy functioned without disruption. Everything moved as it should.

At night, the mirror received brief acknowledgments rather than conversations.

Timing matters, he said once.

The mirror reflected agreement without emphasis.

The reunion day arrived quietly.

The resort lay beyond the city's immediate noise, reached by a road that shed traffic gradually. Trees lined the entrance, manicured enough to suggest care, wild enough to resist sterility. The air carried a different weight there, lighter, scented faintly with water and foliage. It encouraged reflection without demanding it.

Guests arrived in clusters. Cars rolled in smoothly, staff directed them efficiently. Sanjay positioned himself near the entrance, greeting arrivals with measured familiarity. He did not linger. He acknowledged presence, then allowed movement.

The atmosphere assembled itself.

Conversations began cautiously, then loosened. Laughter surfaced. Old stories were referenced, reshaped by distance. People compared trajectories subtly, measuring success without announcing it. Sanjay observed quietly, noting who spoke easily, who listened carefully, who scanned rooms for recognition.

Anaya arrived later than most.

She stepped out of her car with confidence practiced over years. Her appearance was composed, deliberate. She scanned the surroundings briefly, then noticed him. Their eyes met without hesitation. She smiled. He returned the gesture with equal ease.

They greeted each other politely. No reference to the past. No acknowledgement of distance. They spoke of the event, of the turnout, of shared acquaintances. Their exchange lasted minutes, ended naturally. She moved on to greet others.

Sanjay did not follow.

As the day progressed, sessions were organized. Discussions framed as professional exchange rather than reminiscence. Panels spoke of industry shifts, of adaptability, of networks. Sanjay participated selectively, offering insights that were practical rather than aspirational. His words carried weight without emphasis.

People listened.

During a break, he stood alone near the terrace, watching the landscape settle into afternoon. The resort's design encouraged separation as much as gathering. Paths curved gently, inviting movement without confrontation. Water reflected light unevenly.

Anaya approached him again, this time without buffer.

"You've built something," she said, glancing around.

He nodded. "It works."

She hesitated, then continued. "You always were disciplined."

He acknowledged the observation without response.

They stood in silence briefly. It was not uncomfortable. It was conclusive.

Later, during an informal gathering arranged deliberately without agenda, Sanjay spoke.

He did not raise his voice. He did not command attention. He waited until conversations softened naturally, then addressed the group without ceremony. He spoke about misjudgment, about offering more than was measured, about learning through restraint. He did not frame it as confession. He framed it as acknowledgment.

He did not name Anaya. He did not need to.

His words were precise. They carried finality without accusation. They closed a chapter publicly without dramatizing it.

Anaya listened without reaction. She understood. Others sensed something had concluded without fully grasping what.

The moment passed.

The gathering continued.

That evening, as guests departed gradually, Sanjay remained attentive without fatigue. He thanked people. He listened to compliments without absorbing them. He ensured departures were smooth.

When the resort finally quieted, he stood alone briefly in the empty hall. The air carried the residue of voices that had mattered and then dispersed. He did not feel relief. He felt alignment.

At home that night, the mirror reflected a face unburdened by explanation.

That part is closed, he said.

The mirror did not respond.

The invitation had done its work. Not as lure, not as spectacle, but as convergence. It had gathered threads without tension, positioned narratives without confrontation.

Sanjay turned off the light and returned to routine, aware that this was not an ending. It was placement.

What followed would require less preparation.

And far less patience.

Chapter Fourteen

The House That Remembered

The estate lay beyond the limits of familiarity, far enough from daily traffic to feel insulated from correction. The road that led to it narrowed gradually, shedding noise and urgency as it progressed. Trees grew closer there, older, their branches forming uneven canopies that filtered light into fragments. The air felt denser, carrying the smell of damp earth and long-kept stone.

The house appeared without announcement. It did not rise dramatically. It revealed itself slowly, its proportions measured, its walls thick with a permanence that resisted renovation. This was not a structure that sought admiration. It expected acknowledgment. Generations had passed through it, altering details but never intention. The building held memory the way soil held moisture, invisible but persistent.

Sanjay arrived alone in the late afternoon. He parked at a distance, choosing to walk the remaining stretch. The gravel underfoot shifted slightly with each step, producing a sound that did not echo. The house absorbed noise easily. It had learned to.

He stood before the entrance for a moment longer than required. Not out of hesitation, but recognition. This place had shaped narratives long before he had language to question them. Decisions made inside these walls had traveled outward, altering lives without ever leaving marks on the surface.

The doors were unlocked. They always were.

Inside, the air was cool, even in summer. Thick walls preserved temperature and silence with equal efficiency. The main hall stretched wide, its ceiling supported by beams darkened by time. Furniture remained arranged according to patterns no one remembered establishing. Chairs faced inward, encouraging assembly. Windows admitted light reluctantly, as if rationing exposure.

Sanjay moved through rooms methodically. He checked arrangements without appearing to. He noted exits, corridors, stairwells. The house was generous in size but conservative in movement. It guided people subtly, narrowing options without announcing them.

The gathering had been scheduled carefully. Relatives would arrive at staggered times, their entrances spread across hours rather than minutes. No single moment would attract attention. No single arrival would dominate. The house preferred accumulation.

The first to arrive were those who always arrived early, mistaking punctuality for virtue. They greeted the space familiarly, commenting on maintenance, on changes, on what had not changed. Their voices carried entitlement softened by nostalgia.

More followed. Brothers. Sisters. Cousins. Eight of them in total, spread across branches that had flourished differently but shared confidence in inheritance. They arrived with spouses, with children, with the assurance of those who believed the house belonged to them regardless of documentation.

They greeted Sanjay with measured politeness. Some smiled too easily. Others offered warmth that did not reach their eyes. No one questioned why he had arranged the gathering. That question implied scrutiny. They preferred assumption.

Conversations filled the hall gradually. Topics remained light at first. Health. Travel. Developments in the city. Comparisons disguised as interest. Stories retold with adjustments that favored repetition over accuracy.

Sanjay moved among them quietly, offering greetings without attachment. He listened more than he spoke. When he spoke, his words were neutral, difficult to reinterpret. He observed how they clustered instinctively, how alliances formed without announcement. The same patterns from years earlier reappeared unchanged.

They spoke of his father occasionally, with restraint that suggested caution rather than respect. His mother's name surfaced rarely, and when it did, it carried undertones that required no elaboration. Sanjay noted each instance without reaction.

As evening approached, the house adjusted its tone. Shadows lengthened. The light inside grew softer, more deceptive. Lamps were switched on one by one, illuminating sections rather than the whole. The building preferred partial visibility.

Food was arranged in the adjoining room, laid out generously. The smell of spices traveled through corridors, drawing people together. They ate standing, plates balanced, conversations loosening under the influence of familiarity and comfort. Laughter surfaced, genuine in places, performative in others.

Sanjay remained attentive. He ensured nothing appeared rushed. Timing mattered.

When the house was full and the night had settled, he spoke.

He did not raise his voice. He did not seek attention. He allowed the room to find quiet naturally, the way it always had when something important was about to be decided. Conversations tapered. Plates were set aside. People turned toward him without instruction.

He stood near the center of the hall, not elevated, not hidden. The light reached him unevenly, casting shadows that softened edges. He did not introduce himself. Everyone knew who he was.

He spoke of family responsibility. Of how houses survived not on walls but on agreements. He spoke of care, of continuity, of the costs of misinterpretation. His words were careful, chosen for accuracy rather than comfort. He did not accuse. He did not defend.

He spoke of narratives.

He said that stories, once established, outlived those who told them. That they traveled freely, attaching themselves to convenience. That families often mistook repetition for truth. His voice remained steady. His gaze moved deliberately, meeting eyes without challenge.

Some shifted uncomfortably. Others remained still, confident in their version of events.

He spoke of his mother.

He did not describe her. He did not recount illness or sacrifice. He said only that she had wanted family, not property. That she had entered this house without ambition. That what she had received instead was interpretation.

The room remained silent.

He did not linger on the point. He did not allow emotion to swell. He spoke of his father's years of responsibility, of how work done without recognition often became invisible once it was no longer useful. He did not name individuals. He did not need to.

The house listened.

Some relatives exchanged glances. A few attempted to smile, to soften what felt like exposure. Others waited, assuming this would pass as other moments had.

Sanjay concluded without flourish. He said nothing that could be quoted easily. Nothing that could be reduced. He allowed ambiguity to remain, knowing that clarity would arrive later.

The gathering resumed slowly. Conversations restarted, quieter now. People moved differently, aware of something having shifted without fully understanding how. Some approached Sanjay afterward, offering reassurance, explanations, deflections. He accepted them politely, offering nothing in return.

As the night deepened, fatigue set in. Children grew restless. Adults excused themselves gradually, departures spreading out as arrivals had. Cars left the drive quietly, headlights cutting briefly through trees before disappearing.

When the house emptied, it did not return to silence immediately. It held the residue of voices, the echo of certainty disrupted. Sanjay walked through rooms again, slower this time. The walls absorbed everything without comment.

He stood once more in the main hall, now dimly lit. The house felt heavier, as if something had been added rather than removed.

At home later that night, he stood before the mirror. The light was low. His reflection appeared calm, unchanged.

They heard it, he said.

The mirror did not respond.

Whether they understood did not matter. Understanding was not required for consequence.

He turned off the light and returned to his room. Outside, the city settled into sleep. Inside, a house older than memory held what it had been given.

The gathering had ended.

The house remembered.

Chapter Fifteen

Fire Without Witness

The night did not announce itself with wind or thunder. It arrived quietly, folding itself around the estate as it always had, patient and unremarkable. The house settled into its familiar posture, absorbing darkness the way it absorbed voices, without resistance and without release. Lamps were switched off in stages. Corridors dimmed. The building returned to its preferred state, half-seen, half-remembered.

Sanjay remained after the last car had left, not moving immediately, not listening for echoes. He waited for the house to decide it was alone again. That moment arrived without sound. It always did.

He walked through rooms slowly, not searching, not checking, simply moving as if counting steps that had already been memorized. Floors responded with muted acknowledgment. Doors remained where they had always been. Nothing demanded attention. That, he understood, was the house's talent. It did not distract. It accepted.

In the kitchen, the air retained the residue of food and warmth, traces of comfort that would soon dissipate. He paused there briefly, his hand resting on the counter, his gaze unfixed. The room had served its purpose. It would do so again in other hands, on other nights, until it did not.

He moved on.

Outside, the grounds were still. Trees stood unmoved. The gravel path lay undisturbed. The sky offered no signal. Even insects seemed to keep their distance, as if sensing a threshold that did not require crossing.

The act itself did not feel like action. It felt like sequence.

Sanjay did not hurry. Haste invited error. Error invited story. He had learned long ago that narratives survived mistakes better than they survived precision. He allowed each step to complete itself before beginning the next.

The house did not resist.

When the first sign of change occurred, it was internal. A shift in temperature that did not announce itself as danger. A subtle imbalance, felt rather than observed. The building adjusted, as structures often did, compensating quietly for forces they had not been designed to accommodate.

Sanjay did not remain to watch.

He exited the grounds by the same path he had entered, his movements unremarkable, his pace steady. The gate closed behind him with a sound that did not echo. The lane beyond curved gently, concealing the estate from immediate view. He did not turn back.

By the time the change became visible, it belonged to others.

Light appeared where it had not been before, uneven, uncontained. It flickered briefly, uncertain, then grew more confident, asserting itself against stone and wood that had endured for decades. Smoke followed, hesitant at first, then purposeful, finding pathways the house had never intended to offer.

Those nearby noticed eventually. Someone pointed. Someone shouted. Phones emerged. Vehicles slowed. The night, once unremarkable, adjusted its tone.

The fire did not behave theatrically. It did not roar. It did not collapse the structure immediately. It worked methodically, consuming what it found available, respecting density, testing resistance. The house responded as it had been built to, containing spread, delaying consequence. That resistance extended the moment, allowed confusion to gather.

By the time emergency services arrived, the estate had already made its decision.

Lights cut through smoke. Voices layered over one another. Instructions were issued and repeated. Water met flame where it could reach. Heat retreated in places, advanced in others. The building offered no clarity. It concealed as much as it revealed.

Neighbors gathered at a distance, held back by barriers and instinct. They watched without speaking much, recording fragments without context. The night filled with controlled urgency, the kind that arrived too late to alter origin.

Sanjay was not there.

He returned home before dawn, his route familiar, his arrival unremarked. The house greeted him with routine. His mother slept lightly, her breath measured. His father's room remained dark. The neighborhood remained intact, unaware of the adjustment occurring elsewhere.

He washed his hands carefully, the way he always did, the ritual unchanged by circumstance. Cleanliness was habit, not absolution. He did not linger at the sink. He dried his hands and moved on.

Sleep arrived without negotiation.

Morning brought confirmation.

News traveled faster than explanation. A fire at the old estate. Damage extensive. Casualties uncertain. Officials cautious in their statements. Causes under review. The language was familiar, practiced, designed to occupy space without offering conclusion.

Photographs circulated. The house appeared altered, sections darkened, windows hollowed, stone blackened unevenly. Smoke lingered in the air, clinging to memory as much as material.

Names began to surface.

Relatives were listed. Attendance was confirmed retroactively. Phone calls multiplied. Messages arrived without sequence. Shock adopted familiar forms. Grief assembled itself unevenly.

Sanjay listened without interruption.

At home, his mother sensed the shift before being told. She noticed the way the house held its breath, the way voices on the television carried a different weight. When Sanjay explained briefly, she closed her eyes and nodded. She did not ask questions that required answers. Her body conserved energy for what it could endure.

His father remained quiet. He read the reports carefully, noting phrasing, omissions, emphasis. He did not comment. He did not speculate. He folded the paper and set it aside.

The city responded predictably. Officials visited the site. Statements were issued. The fire was described as accident pending investigation. Electrical fault was mentioned. Structural age noted. Maintenance records questioned gently. No accusation gained traction.

The house had been old.

The house had been full.

The house had been vulnerable.

These were sufficient explanations.

Police visited homes, asked routine questions, documented presence and absence. When they arrived at Sanjay's, their demeanor remained formal. They noted timelines, confirmed addresses, recorded statements that offered nothing beyond fact. Sanjay answered clearly, without embellishment, without delay.

They left with nothing to carry.

In offices, files were opened and closed. The incident was categorized. Procedures were followed. Oversight was applied where required. The event entered the system and began its transformation into record.

Sanjay observed the process from a distance that felt appropriate.

At night, the mirror reflected a face that did not search for justification. He stood before it briefly, his posture aligned, his expression neutral.

They will call it accident, he said.

The mirror did not contradict him.

He continued, quieter now. They will call it tragedy.

Tragedy, he understood, was a word that allowed endings without responsibility.

He turned away from the mirror and returned to routine.

The days that followed unfolded with measured gravity. Funerals were arranged. Attendance was recorded. Words were spoken that sought closure rather than truth. Sanjay attended when expected, stood where required, spoke only when addressed. His presence did not draw attention. It did not need to.

Some relatives looked at him longer than necessary. Others avoided his gaze entirely. No one accused. Accusation required certainty. Certainty had not survived the fire.

Rumours attempted to form and failed. There were too many witnesses, too many variables, too much official language occupying space. Stories dissolved before they could stabilize.

The narrative that had lived for years lost its carriers.

Sanjay noticed the absence gradually. Conversations that once hovered now fell silent. Names were mentioned less often. Interpretations lost their audience. What remained were records, procedures, outcomes.

At home, life continued.

His mother rested more. Her illness demanded attention. Sanjay adjusted schedules, managed care, maintained order. His father remained present, his routines unchanged, his silence intact.

The house remained steady.

Weeks passed.

The investigation concluded quietly. Findings were released without emphasis. The fire was ruled accidental. The estate was deemed unsafe. The land entered a different category, subject to process, valuation, redistribution. The cycle resumed under new conditions.

Sanjay did not involve himself.

At night, the mirror received no words now. The conversations had concluded. There was nothing left to measure, nothing left to place.

The fire had done what confrontation never could.

It had erased the house that held the story.

And with it, the voices that kept repeating it.

Sanjay turned off the light and lay down. Outside, the city returned to routine. Inside, the silence felt complete, not as relief, but as resolution.

The fire had not demanded confession.

Neither would he.

Chapter Sixteen

No Arrest

The city adjusted itself cautiously in the days that followed. It did not grieve publicly. It processed. Offices opened on time. Buses followed routes without deviation. People spoke of the fire in lowered voices, careful to keep distance between fact and speculation. The event occupied space in conversation briefly, then settled into the background where unresolved things often lived.

Police stations carried the smell of paper and disinfectant, unchanged by tragedy. Files were logged. Statements were cross-referenced. Timelines were assembled with precision that suggested confidence while avoiding commitment. Officers worked methodically, not out of urgency but habit. The system preferred rhythm over resolution.

Sanjay became aware of their attention not through confrontation but through presence. An officer appeared once near the restaurant, ordering tea, observing the room without announcing purpose. Another visited the consultancy office, asking questions framed as verification rather than suspicion. They were polite. They were thorough. They were cautious.

When they finally arrived at his house formally, it was mid-morning. The sun had already settled into its position, casting predictable light across the front room. His mother rested in the adjacent space, her breathing measured. His father sat at the table, reading, the newspaper folded precisely at the same angle it always was.

The officers introduced themselves without emphasis. Names were exchanged. Notebooks opened. Questions followed.

Where had he been that night. What time had he left the estate. Who had seen him afterward. What route had he taken home.

Sanjay answered without delay. His responses were factual, stripped of narrative. He did not volunteer detail beyond what was requested. He did not hesitate, which would have invited interpretation. He did not rush, which would have suggested anxiety.

The officers wrote carefully.

They asked about family relations. He answered neutrally. They asked about recent gatherings. He confirmed attendance. They asked about disputes. He acknowledged none that were unresolved.

They noted the presence of his parents. They observed the house. They did not ask about his mother directly. Illness required delicacy, and delicacy slowed inquiry.

Before leaving, one officer paused, looking around the room as if expecting something to reveal itself. Nothing did.

They thanked him and left.

In the following weeks, similar visits occurred elsewhere. Relatives were questioned. Neighbours were interviewed. Resort staff were contacted. Officials compiled information that resisted assembly into accusation. Each account was correct. Each timeline aligned. No contradictions surfaced that demanded pursuit.

The problem was not lack of suspicion. It was excess of plausibility.

The fire had too many explanations. Electrical faults. Structural decay. Human negligence without intent. The estate's age worked against precision. Its design resisted forensic clarity. Smoke had erased details that might have mattered. Water had completed the work.

The police understood this. They had seen it before. Certain cases arrived already concluded by circumstance.

Still, caution demanded distance.

Sanjay noticed the shift in tone gradually. Initial attentiveness softened into routine. Officers stopped visiting. Inquiries slowed. Files moved from desks to cabinets. The case entered a category that did not invite urgency.

There was no announcement of closure. There rarely was.

In public spaces, people watched him differently for a time. Glances lingered slightly longer. Conversations paused when he entered rooms, then resumed cautiously. Suspicion attempted to form but found no structure to attach itself to.

He continued his routines unchanged.

The restaurant functioned smoothly. Customers returned. Conversations resumed their usual patterns. No one mentioned the fire openly. When it was mentioned, it was framed as misfortune rather than event. Sanjay did not contribute. He listened.

At the consultancy, work continued uninterrupted. Files were processed. Disputes resolved. Officials interacted with him as before, neither warmer nor colder. Procedure did not accommodate conjecture.

In Mysore, reputation did not collapse suddenly. It eroded only when repeated contradiction appeared. Sanjay offered none.

His mother's health required more attention now. The strain of recent weeks manifested physically. Sanjay adjusted his schedule, staying home more often, delegating responsibilities without relinquishing control. He ensured comfort, consistency, silence where needed.

His father observed all of this without remark. One evening, he spoke only once.

"Things end quietly," he said, as if reading aloud rather than commenting.

Sanjay nodded. He did not ask what he meant.

At night, the mirror reflected a face that no longer required dialogue. Sanjay stood before it briefly, not to speak but to confirm. His posture remained aligned. His expression neutral.

Fear had not arrived. Fear required uncertainty. This phase was defined by clarity.

Weeks passed.

The investigation concluded without ceremony. Reports were filed. Causes were attributed. The estate was listed as unsafe. Access was restricted. Future decisions would be administrative rather than emotional.

The police did not return.

No arrest was made. No charge was filed. No suspicion matured into accusation.

The absence of action did not feel like victory. Victory implied contest. This felt like closure achieved through inevitability.

Sanjay attended required functions. He stood through rituals that marked loss without examining cause. He spoke when addressed. He listened when spoken to. He maintained presence without offering narrative.

Some relatives avoided him now. Others approached cautiously, seeking reassurance without asking questions. He offered neither reassurance nor distance. He allowed interactions to define themselves.

The family story that had once circulated so confidently no longer found listeners. Its carriers had diminished. Those who remained found repetition exhausting rather than empowering. Silence replaced assertion.

At home, the house remained orderly. Meals were prepared. Medicines administered. Routines preserved. The domestic world continued, unaffected by external resolution.

Sanjay understood then that the absence of arrest was not a failure of justice. It was the outcome of alignment. Every system had behaved according to its nature. He had anticipated that nature and adjusted himself accordingly.

In the mirror, one final sentence formed without sound.

There is nothing left to answer.

He turned away from the glass and returned to his room. Outside, the city moved on, its memory selective, its attention finite.

Inside, the silence held.

No arrest had been made.

And nothing remained to pursue.

Chapter Seventeen

What Remained

The days after certainty did not arrive as relief. They arrived as continuity. Morning followed night with the same indifference it always had, and Sanjay understood then that endings were rarely marked by change in rhythm. They were marked by the absence of disturbance.

The house returned to its patterns quickly. His mother woke late, her body moving slower now, as if conserving itself for what it could no longer afford to waste. Sanjay prepared her meals carefully, adjusting textures, timing medicines with precision. He spoke to her gently, never urgently. Illness required calm more than reassurance.

She did not ask about the fire again. She had heard enough to understand that questions would not produce answers she could use. She focused instead on what was immediate. The temperature of tea. The placement of pillows. The sound of birds in the morning. These were things that remained available.

His father resumed his routines without interruption. Newspapers were read thoroughly. Articles were folded with care. Sometimes he paused longer at certain reports, those involving accidents, disputes, closures. He did not comment. He had learned long ago that language often failed to contain truth without damaging it.

Sanjay observed both of them with the same attentiveness he applied to everything else. He did not hover. He did not withdraw. He placed himself where he was needed and remained there without announcement.

Outside, the world adjusted.

The estate was fenced off. Signs were posted. The land entered administrative uncertainty, its future suspended between valuation and redistribution. People spoke of it occasionally, but without the intimacy that once fueled narrative. It had become property again, stripped of voice.

Relatives dispersed into their separate lives. Some relocated. Others retreated into routine. Gatherings ceased. Phone calls dwindled. The connective tissue that had once carried stories dissolved quietly.

Sanjay noticed how quickly people adapted to silence once repetition lost purpose.

At the restaurant, customers returned to familiar conversations. The fire surfaced briefly in recollection, then faded. New topics replaced it. Local concerns. Prices. Weather. Plans. The space absorbed normalcy efficiently.

At the consultancy, work continued uninterrupted. Files were resolved. New disputes arrived. Old ones closed. Sanjay handled them with the same restraint as before. Nothing in his professional demeanor changed. That consistency mattered more than explanation.

Officials interacted with him as they always had. With caution. With respect. Without curiosity.

He understood then that his position had solidified not because of what had happened, but because nothing after it contradicted what people already believed about him. Reputation survived on confirmation, not event.

The mirror returned to being an object rather than a witness.

Days passed without conversation. Sanjay still stood before it occasionally, not to speak but to observe alignment. His face carried no triumph. It carried completion.

There were moments when memory surfaced unexpectedly. A sound. A smell. A phrase repeated by someone unaware of its history. These moments did not wound him. They passed through him like data, acknowledged and stored without emotion.

Pain had not disappeared. It had been placed.

One evening, his mother asked him to sit beside her longer than usual. Her voice was softer, her breath shallow. The room held the smell of medicine and evening air. She looked at him without urgency.

"You are tired," she said.

He did not deny it. He did not explain.

She rested her hand on his briefly, the contact light but intentional. "You have done enough," she said, not as instruction but as recognition.

Sanjay nodded. He did not interpret the words beyond their offering.

Later that night, after she slept, he sat alone in the front room. The television was off. The house held its quiet without tension. He thought of his father years earlier, seated at a table, files arranged carefully, responsibility carried without witness.

He understood then that inheritance did not always arrive through property or name. Sometimes it arrived through repetition of restraint.

The fire had removed a structure. It had not created chaos. It had redistributed silence.

Sanjay did not regret. Regret implied alternative desire. He had not acted out of desire. He had acted out of inevitability shaped by observation.

He slept without disturbance.

Morning returned.

The city continued.

What remained was not guilt or satisfaction. It was order.

Order in a life once distorted by narrative. Order in a house once subjected to rumor. Order in memory, which no longer demanded defense.

Sanjay rose and prepared breakfast. He arranged his mother's medicine. He checked schedules. He reviewed messages. He proceeded.

There was nothing left to correct.

Only to continue.

Chapter Eighteen

He Does Not Confess

Morning arrived without emphasis. Light entered the house slowly, settling on familiar surfaces, tracing edges it had traced countless times before. The ceiling fan turned at its usual pace. The street outside released its first sounds reluctantly, a vehicle passing, a voice calling, life assembling itself without regard for what had concluded elsewhere.

Sanjay woke before the house did. He lay still for a moment, listening, not for disturbance but for alignment. Everything sounded as it should.

He rose and walked to the bathroom. The mirror waited, unchanged, its surface carrying no memory of the years it had witnessed. Steam from the previous night had faded. The glass was clear.

He looked at himself for a long moment.

There was no question left to ask.

In the early years, the mirror had been a place of measurement. Later, it had become a place of confirmation. Now it was only reflection. He did not speak. Words would have suggested unfinished thought.

He washed his face, dried his hands, adjusted his shirt. Small corrections. Habitual precision. The kind that required no explanation.

In the kitchen, water heated. Tea leaves steeped. Breakfast followed the pattern that had sustained the house for years. His mother woke slowly, her body taking longer now to assemble itself into readiness. He helped her sit, placed the cup in her hands, adjusted the pillow behind her back.

She watched him quietly.

"You slept," she said.

"Yes," he replied.

She nodded. That was enough.

His father entered later, newspaper already folded under his arm, his movements unchanged despite the years that had passed. He sat at the table, adjusted the chair, unfolded the paper. The rustle of pages filled the room briefly, then settled.

No one spoke of the past.

Outside, the city continued its ordinary negotiations. Shops opened. Offices prepared. Files waited. Somewhere, the land where the estate had stood remained fenced, its future suspended in paperwork and valuation. It no longer belonged to memory. It belonged to process.

Sanjay left the house at his usual time. He locked the door carefully, tested the latch once, then walked toward the road without looking back. There was nothing behind him that required vigilance.

At the consultancy office, files awaited review. Appointments were scheduled. People arrived carrying disputes they believed urgent. Sanjay listened, clarified, redirected. Systems absorbed conflict and returned resolution where possible. Where resolution was not possible, certainty replaced hope.

At the restaurant, staff moved with confidence born of routine. Orders were taken. Meals were served. Conversations flowed. No one asked questions that mattered beyond the table. The world, he observed, preferred surfaces once deeper currents were no longer stirred.

Occasionally, someone looked at him longer than necessary. Curiosity still existed. It always would. But curiosity without structure faded quickly. Without accusation, without contradiction, it lost momentum.

Police did not return.

No letter arrived.

No summons appeared.

The system had done what systems did. It had categorized, processed, concluded. It required no confession to complete itself.

Sanjay understood that confession was a transaction. It traded silence for narrative, closure for exposure. It invited interpretation, judgment, moral resolution. He had no interest in any of those outcomes.

Confession belonged to those who needed forgiveness or explanation.

He needed neither.

In the weeks that followed, life stabilized further. His mother's health required increasing care, but it remained managed. Some days were more difficult than others. Pain arrived unpredictably, receded with treatment, returned without warning. Sanjay adjusted constantly, without complaint. Care was not sacrifice. It was responsibility carried correctly.

His father aged quietly, his routines thinning but intact. He spoke little now, conserving words as he had once conserved effort. Sometimes he looked at Sanjay with a recognition that did not require language. Sometimes he said nothing at all.

One evening, as the light outside faded unevenly, his father spoke.

"Stories end," he said, as if reading from memory rather than speaking.

Sanjay looked at him.

"Only when they stop being told," his father continued.

Sanjay nodded. He understood.

Later that night, Sanjay stood once more before the mirror. Not because he needed it, but because habit completed itself best when acknowledged. He looked at his reflection without expectation.

He did not rehearse denial.

He did not prepare explanation.

He did not justify.

There was nothing left to confess.

The pain he had carried had been measured, placed, and contained. It no longer pressed against speech. It no longer demanded release. It had become part of structure, not emotion.

Outside, the city prepared for another day. Inside, the house settled into sleep, its rooms holding silence that no longer felt heavy.

Sanjay lay down without resistance. Sleep arrived naturally, without interruption.

The next morning would arrive as this one had. Light would enter. Routine would resume. Life would continue without acknowledgement of what had been resolved beneath its surface.

He would wake.

He would work.

He would care.

He would remain.

And if anyone ever asked him what had happened, if anyone ever suggested that truth required declaration, he would answer as he always had.

With precision.

With restraint.

With silence.

He does not confess.

Epilogue

Ash Settles Quietly

Time did what it always did. It softened edges without correcting shape.

The land where the estate had stood was cleared eventually. Charred stone was removed piece by piece, catalogued as debris, transported without ceremony. What remained was soil disturbed and then leveled, its surface reset by machines that did not know what they erased. Fencing stayed longer than necessary, a gesture toward caution rather than memory. Eventually even that was taken down.

People stopped pointing when they passed the place. Directions changed. The absence integrated itself into routine.

In offices, the matter existed only as reference. A file number. A closed inquiry. An example cited briefly when someone asked about safety standards or old wiring. The tone was always neutral. The past did not require emotion to remain instructive.

Within the family, silence completed what distance had begun. Some moved away. Others rebuilt smaller lives around safer certainties. The old confidence that had once animated gatherings did not return. Without the house, there was nowhere for it to assemble. Without repetition, the story lost coherence.

No one apologized.

No one accused.

That, Sanjay understood, was how resolution often arrived.

At home, life narrowed into essentials. His mother's health demanded increasing attention. The days became shaped around her comfort, her breath, her rest. Sanjay adjusted his work without announcing sacrifice. He delegated where necessary, withdrew where possible. The systems he had built absorbed his absence without collapse.

Care became quieter, more precise. He learned the sound of her discomfort before she spoke. He learned which silences were restful and which required intervention. He learned how much of life could be carried without words.

His father faded gradually, not into absence but into stillness. He spent more time by the window, watching light shift across familiar ground. Sometimes he spoke of nothing. Sometimes he spoke of work long finished, names long forgotten. Sanjay listened without correction. Memory did not require accuracy to remain meaningful.

The mirror in the bathroom remained where it had always been. It reflected mornings and nights without judgment. Sanjay stood before it less often now. When he did, it was only to adjust posture, to correct alignment. The conversations had ended. The witness had been released.

The restaurant continued. The consultancy endured. Buildings stood where plans had once existed only on paper. Reputation settled into something quieter than recognition. People trusted him without needing to know him. That distance suited him.

Occasionally, someone mentioned the fire again, usually as anecdote, stripped of weight. Sanjay listened politely. He did not correct timelines. He did not add detail. He allowed the version to remain as it was told. Stories weakened when no one defended or opposed them.

Years passed without marker.

Sanjay did not measure his life against what had been taken or what had been done. Measurement implied comparison, and comparison invited judgment. He preferred calibration. Things worked or they did not. Pain existed or it did not. Most of the time, it existed quietly, no longer demanding response.

On an ordinary evening, as the city settled into routine, Sanjay sat beside his mother, holding her hand lightly. Her breath was shallow but steady. The room carried the familiar smells of medicine and evening air. She looked at him for a long moment.

"You are calm," she said.

He nodded.

That was all.

Later, after she slept, Sanjay stood alone in the front room. The house was silent, not expectant, not heavy. Just quiet. He looked around at walls that had never held lies loudly enough to echo. He understood then that home was not where one was protected from harm, but where harm no longer needed explanation.

He turned off the light and went to bed.

Outside, the city continued, indifferent and precise. Inside, nothing waited to be said.

Ash had settled.

Silence remained.

And the man who had carried pain without surrender continued living exactly as he had chosen.

Without confession.

9 789357 797696

Printed at Repro India Ltd.